I0547955

Cover illustration by Kathleen C. Jameson

Pack your auger!
We're going ice fishing!

In memory of Willow, our rock star, miniature schnauzer.

Chapter 1: *It's beginning to look a lot like Christmas*

Lexi, and her cousins Olivia and Abby were best friends and loved to see each other when they stayed at their cabins at Long Lake near Vergas, Minnesota.

They had just said good-bye to each other after spending Thanksgiving with the whole 50-something Jonsrud clan. Now, Abby and Olivia were at their cabin before they packed up to go home.

"Olivia! Did you KNOWWWWWWW? I have a Christmas gift for Grandma Jonsrud already!" yelled nine-year old Abby at her sister even though they were sitting together on the couch.

Startled, Olivia, Abby's 11-year-old brown-eyed and black-haired sister, looked up from the book that she was reading and shook her head back and forth.

"Geez Abby--will you please use your indoor cabin voice?" Olivia responded, delivering it with just the right hint of irritation that only a big sister can give.

"And that's great that you have Grandma's gift already, but it's just the end of November so I have plenty of time to make a Christmas gift for Grandma too," Olivia added. "You know that I just need to concentrate on doing it."

Abby rolled her eyes, shrugged her shoulders and effortlessly launched into a vertical leap that would impress any high school basketball coach.

Olivia was reading a book about the Vikings and their long history in the Minnesota area. No, not the professional football team, but real Norwegian and Swedish Vikings—the real deal.

Now thinking about Christmas and the gifts she needed to make instead of reading her book, Olivia stared out the cabin's big windows to the quiet, silvery and deep blue water of Long Lake. Her active mind then switched to think about the coming winter. She turned and looked at her brown-eyed and black-haired sister.

"Wow, Abby, the lake is so smooth and cold, I bet it will soon freeze over," Olivia said as she shivered at the thought even though their log cabin--called Junior--was toasty warm.

Junior was a funny name for a cabin. Grandma Jonsrud had named the girls' cabin Junior because it was half the size of Grandma's log cabin on the other side of the lake. The cousins then named Grandma's log cabin "Senior" because Grandma was the oldest in the family and her cabin was the biggest and oldest of the Jonsruds' three lake homes on Long Lake, Minnesota.

Ask-a-cuz: What and where is Long Lake at Vergas?
According the Minnesota Department of Natural Resources, Long Lake is one of 11,842 lakes in Minnesota. Wow. That's a lot of lakes. In Minnesota, a body of water is called a lake if it is at least 10 acres in size. Long Lake at Vergas is 1,273 acres. It is about seven miles long and a mile wide.   Folks around there are whimsical and creative--but sometimes not in the way in which they name lakes. Long Lake at Vergas is one of 10 lakes in Ottertail County with that same name.

The Jonsruds were funny that way. At least they thought they were funny. They laughed hard at their own jokes because their Grandpa once told them that the secret to a good joke was to laugh first and hardest at their own punch line and then others will laugh too.

"Now wait. Wait a minute," Abby said as she rubbed the golden ears of Dakota, their Labrador Retriever.

"Are you telling me—Olivia--that you know when a lake will turn to ice," Abby asked. "I mean you know when it will freeze over. You know--completely?"

Olivia turned toward her sister. Unconsciously and fluidly, Olivia stretched her arms over her head and bent at the waist like a young yoga master.

"Well, I cannot exactly tell you when it will turn to ice, Abby. I can just see that it is very close to turning to ice," Olivia said as she moved into tree pose.

As she balanced, Olivia chose her words carefully because that's just the way the deep-thinking Olivia was.

"You just watch," she said, "I bet in a week or so, the lake will freeze over.

Ask-a-cuz: How does lake water change to ice?

According to Pitara kids network (http://www.pitara.com/discover/5wh/online.asp?story=25) article "How do fish survive in ice waters?" during winter months in Minnesota and other cold states, the air temperature drops to below freezing and the top layers of lake water starts cooling.

When the lake's surface temperature falls to about 39 degrees Fahrenheit, the surface layer of water gets dense or heavy and sinks down. As that layer of water sinks down, it displaces warmer water below. The warmer lower layers of water rise up to the surface. There, the cold air cools the water to 39 degrees and again the heavy, cold water sinks down.

When the temperature of all the water layers goes below 39 degrees, the water layers stop sinking. The surface water finally freezes at 32 degrees while the lower part remains above that freezing mark.

The frozen layer floats on top of the water and there is a pocket of air between the water and the ice (that helps fish to live).

The water below doesn't completely freeze because the ice does not allow heat to pass through it easily. In a normal Minnesota winter, the thickness of the ice on lakes is about 2 feet thick. The ice is thick and strong enough for people to walk and drive vehicles on it.

"Oh ho-ho-ho Dakota, my buddy, my buddy, my buddy!" Abby giggled and grabbed Dakota's head between her hands.

"Olivia may be smart but I think she's trying to pull a joke on us," she said in a sing-songy voice. Abby jumped off the couch and pretended to dribble a basketball and fake out competitors as she moved to the window.

"Well, Oli-vi-ahhhhh, we will see about that. I'm going to ask Uncle Terry to tell us when the lake freezes over," Abby said.

Abby pretended to make a "nothing but net" shot into an imaginary basketball hoop.

"Uncle Terry is always watching for the freeze so he can start ice fishing," Abby said.

"But enough about the lake--take a look at my gift for Grandma," she said, switching topics abruptly as she took a single big leap back to the couch.

Abby reached below the couch and pulled out a towel, upon which lay a large round rock with a smooth, one-inch triangular hole. The hole was about four inches deep in the rock. Abby handed the heavy rock to Olivia.

Olivia sat down on the couch to hold the rock and turned it over a number of times, but did not say anything. She just kept turning it over and looking at the rock.

"Ah, gee whiz Olivia—quit staring at it. It's just a candle holder. Any dude can see that!" Abby said with her hands turned out at her sides to emphasize her point.

The word "dude" was Abby's favorite new word and she used it often lately.

"Where did you find it Abby?" Olivia asked quietly, still staring at the rock.

"I found it near the stairway down to the lakeshore, when I was digging earlier today," Abby said. "Why--what's up?"

Abby sat down next to her sister to look more closely at her rock. She wanted to toss it in the air to catch because she could think better when she played catch, but the rock was too heavy, and besides, her mom didn't want her playing catch in the house—especially with a rock!

"Well, let me show you the book that I'm reading. Your candle holder may be something else from a long time ago," Olivia said excitedly.

Olivia opened her book for Abby and pointed to a picture of a Viking mooring stone. The caption described what mooring stones looked like and said that many had been found in North America, especially in the Minnesota area.

"Well, wait, wait a minute Olivia," Abby said and put her hands on her hips and tapped her right foot. Abby wasn't sure what she wasn't really disagreeing with her sister, but she wanted to slow down the conversation so she could think about the significance of her candle holder or mooring stone.

"Well, so okay, maybe it is a mooring stone," Abby conceded. "But really dude. What the heck is a mooring stone?"

"Vikings used to dig a hole in a rock on the shore and then tie their boat—or moor it—to the rock to keep their boat from floating away," Olivia explained. "Your rock is quite small, but the shape of the hole in it, leads me to think that you have indeed found a piece of a mooring stone!"

The word "indeed" may have been a different word for most Minnesota kids, but Olivia was quite particular in her choice of words.

Ask-a-cuz: What is a mooring stone?
According to Science Frontiers Online at http://www.science-frontiers.com/sf069/sf069a01.htm in its May-June 1990 newsletter, "The enigmatic "mooring stones," archaeologists have pondered the possibility of mooring stones for many years. There are hundreds of rocks with triangular holes in them discovered across Minnesota, North and South Dakota, Illinois, and the Eastern Seaboard.
Some theories say that Vikings moored their boats to the rocks when they visited the area about 1,000 years ago.
In Europe, Norwegian and Swedish fishermen used the technique for hundreds of years to moor their boats on the steep rock walls of fjords. (By the way, a fjord is not a type of car, it is a narrow inlet of sea long the coast of Norway.)

"Well, maybe Olivia, but I think I still want to stick a candle in this one and give it to Grandma as a Christmas gift," Abby said as she placed it back on the towel and slid it back under the couch.

Before Olivia could object, the door opened and the sisters' parents—Beth and Jon—entered the cabin.

"Okay girls, we're a bit late and it's time to pack up. We're going home," their mom said as she petted Dakota. Beth and Jon had just returned from a last walk in the woods before the family headed back to their home near Minneapolis.

"Why can't we just stay here through the holidays?" Olivia moaned. "We love it here."

"Well, my little gal pals," their mom said. "You have to get back to school for a couple of weeks before the Christmas break. And we'll be back before you know it."

You can draw! Draw the sisters looking at the rock with the hole in the middle of it.

Chapter 2: *Grandma gives a history and mystery lesson*

Beth was right. Two weeks passed very quickly. With all their studies and the excitement of the holidays, Olivia and Abby had little time to think about the stone that Abby had found.

During this time, Uncle Terry called and told them that Long Lake had frozen over a few days after Thanksgiving. Olivia had been right with her theory and observation! She made a mental note to remember to trust both research and her intuition.

Now, on a beautiful, but cold, snowy night, Jon, Beth, Olivia, Abby and Dakota drove back to Junior to spend the holidays with the entire Jonsrud family.

"Hey mom, may I use your brand new, 4G, pretty-in-pink, and waterproof cell phone to call Lexi?" Abby asked.

The girls were up on the latest in technology and looks of cell phones.

"And Mom and Dad, you do realize that, if Abby and I had our own cell phones, we could call Lexi ourselves—it would save you the wear and tear of having to hand over your phone to us so often," Olivia injected with a sigh as she sat forward to get closer to her parents in the front seat.

"And did you KNOWWWWWWW that on our school bus there are only three kids who don't have their own phone," Abby added jumping on the bandwagon (or perhaps the school bus).

"And what's even more terrible is that Abby and I are two of those three kids!" Olivia crowed.

"Girls, do we really have to talk about this again," Beth asked as she handed her phone to Abby. "You will get a phone when it's the right time. And I wish you knew that now is not the right time."

"Well, did you KNOWWWWWWW Mom and Dad, that Abby and I would always know the right time if we had a cell phone because it has a clock in it," said Olivia trying another angle.

"Olivia," her Dad said and shot her a look in the rear view mirror.

"Duuude. Guess we don't need a cell phone to pick up that message," Abby muttered under her breath to Olivia.

"Oh hi Aunt Connie—can I talk to Lexi," said Abby shifting gears quickly when Lexi's mom answered the phone. "We're almost to Junior, and Olivia and I want to see Lexi! Oh yeah-- and Merry Christmas!"

A few seconds later, Abby started talking again on the phone.

"Hey Lexi! It's me—Abby. Where are you? Are you at Senior yet? Do you want to sleep at Junior tonight with us? Do you have a Christmas present for Grandma yet? Do you have a Christmas present for me? Oh yeah--and Merry Christmas!"

Abby could almost talk as fast as she could make a fast break layup.

Lexi was Abby and Olivia's lanky, blonde-hair, blue-eyed cousin with whom they often played and solved a number of mysteries around Long Lake, including last summer's "Mystery of the Laughing Loon." At age 12 Lexi was the oldest, tallest, and while she was the most fashion-conscious of the three cousins, she also played basketball, volleyball, soccer, and golf.

"Yes, we're already at Senior with Grandma," Lexi answered the first of Abby's questions.

Lexi was used to being riddled with questions from her inquisitive cousins.

"We just brought in the Christmas tree to warm up before we stick it in a stand in the living room. Right now I'm wrapping Christmas presents that I've made and helping Grandma wrap her presents too," Lexi continued.

"Well, we'll see you soon. We're headed your way, but first we have to stop and heat up Junior," Abby said.

The cousins hung up. Abby, Olivia, and their parents stopped at Junior so that Jon could go in and turn up the furnace.

Abby ran inside with him to grab her present for Grandma so that she could show it to Lexi.

Then the Jonsruds drove the 7 miles or so around to other side of the lake to visit Grandma and Lexi and her family at the Senior cabin while Junior had time to warm up.

Ask-a-cuz: Why does it take a log house time to warm up?
Log homes insulate better than normal wood frame homes because logs are thicker. Because logs are great insulation, it takes awhile for them to cool down or warm up because heat or cold doesn't easily transfer through the logs. So while it takes a bit to warm up a cold cabin, the good news is that once the logs and inside the house are warm, it stays that way for quite awhile even while the air temperature drops outside.

"Hey Lexi, look at this," Abby said as she handed the towel-wrapped rock to Lexi when they were standing next to the beautiful tall, undecorated Norwegian Pine Christmas tree in Grandma's big living room.

Since the rock was wrapped in the towel Lexi didn't realize it was so heavy. The towel slipped from her hands and the rock dropped to the floor with a big bang.

The floor shook.

You could even say it was a clatter.

Before they knew it all the adults had sprung from the kitchen and ran to the living room to see what was the matter.

"Are you girls alright," Grandma asked. Grandma spotted the rock on the floor.

"And where did you find that mooring stone," she added.

"Grandma—you know what it is?" Olivia asked excitedly.

"oh no—ohhhh she doesn't!" Abby moaned. "It's a candle holder for you Grandma."

"And it's a beautiful one Abby," Grandma said. Grandma put her arm around Abby's drooped shoulders. "But I also think it is a mooring stone and if your Grandpa were still here, he would be thrilled with your gift! Where did you find it?"

Abby shows Grandma the mooring stone.

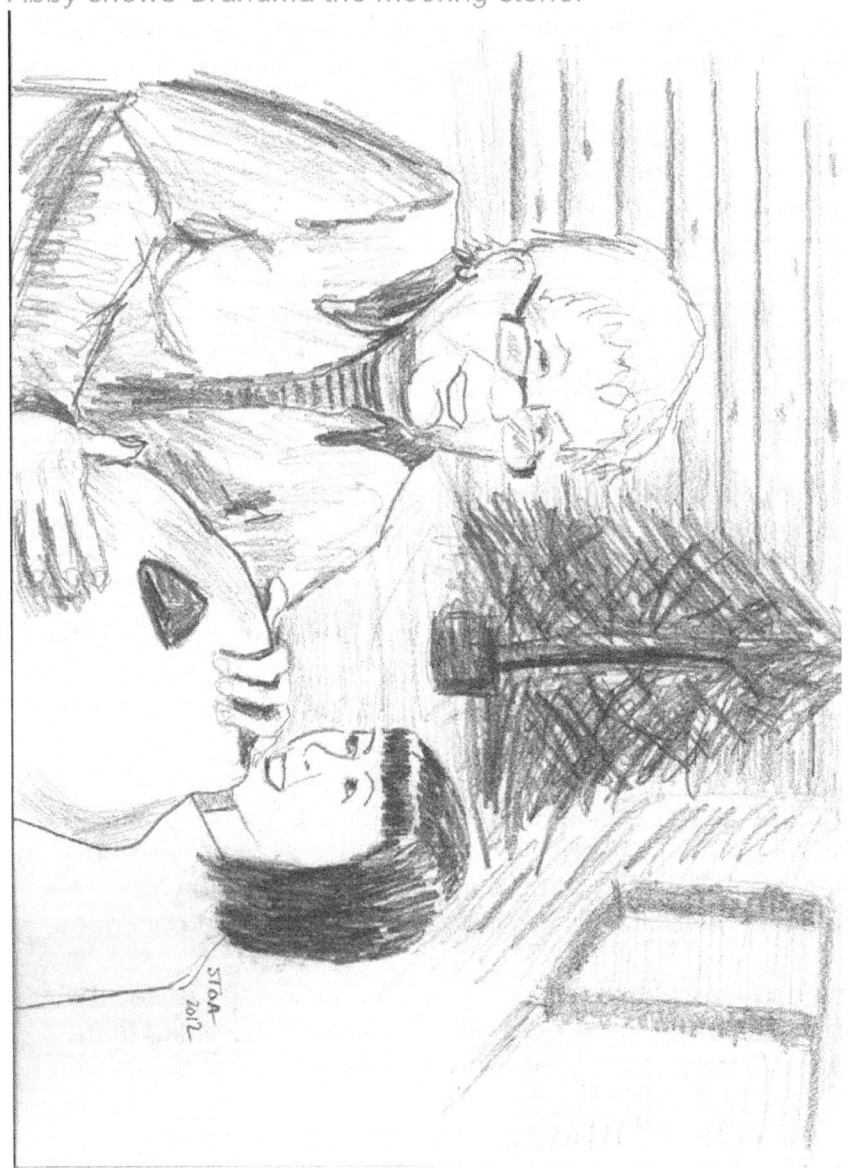

Olivia and Abby had never met Grandpa Jonsrud because he had passed away 13 years ago.

Abby told the group how she had discovered the stone Thanksgiving weekend by the shore on the other side of the lake. And then Olivia filled in the group on the significance of the triangular shape of the hole in the rock.

Like Olivia, Grandma thought the rock was pretty small to be a mooring stone, but reasoned that it had probably broken off from a larger stone and over time, the water had rounded the edges of the rock.

Grandma was excited. She walked into her bedroom and returned in a few minutes, carrying a dusty-covered wooden crate with handles on both sides.

"I haven't opened this box since your grandpa passed away, but I think the time has come for you to learn more about his hobby," Grandma said as she opened the lid of the box, while looking at the cousins and their parents.

"Grandpa spent the last 20 years of his life following clues to days long gone by," she said. "A lot of his audiotapes and notes in this box support the information that Olivia has studied in her books on Vikings' travel," Grandma continued.

"You see, it could have been possible for Vikings to sail their boats all the way here from other continents because there was more water here thousands of years ago," she explained.

The three cousins looked at each other with surprised looks.

"But Grandma—Minnesota is already the land of 10,000 lakes," Olivia said with a gulp. "Do you mean to say that it used to have more lakes than 10,000?"

"Yes, it's true, but let's start back even earlier than that," Grandma said.

"Oh, so you mean before you were born," Lexi commented innocently.

"Lexi!" Grandma said pretending to be shocked. "Of course, it was before I was born. I'm going to tell you a bit about the Ice Age."

Grandma laughed, and then she adjusted her eyeglasses as if it would help her see back in time.

"During the Ice Age this whole area—most of the northern part of North America--was under a huge glacier. When the glacier melted, it receded north and it created a huge lake, called Lake Agassiz. Lake Agassiz was the largest body of fresh water in the world," Grandma explained. "Some say that Lake Agassiz held more water than all of the lakes in the world today."

"Wow, that's big," Lexi said.

Abby didn't say anything but let out a slow whistle. Olivia just scooted up closer to Grandma so that she wouldn't miss a word.

In fact, Grandma's audience was growing; the cousins' parents had pulled up chairs to listen to the story too.

Grandma explained how the glacial lake disappeared about 8,000 to 9,000 years ago, but it left many lakes and rivers in the Minnesota, North Dakota, South Dakota and Wisconsin areas.

"In fact, you know the Red River that runs between Fargo and Moorhead," Grandma asked.

"Yes," answered Lexi. "The Red River separates North Dakota and Minnesota. My teacher says it is the only river in North America that flows north."

"That's right," Grandma said. "Most rivers flow south toward the equator. The reason the Red River flows north is because as both the glacier and then Lake Agassiz receded, they cut a path in the earth that drops slowly lower in elevation as it goes north.

"So Grandma," Lexi jumped in again. "Did the glacier and Lake Agassiz form the Red River Valley?"

"You are right again, Lexi, Very good!" Grandma said and gave Lexi a "high five."

Not to be outdone, Olivia said, "Well Grandma, I believe the Red River Valley is known as one of the most fertile places in the world for agriculture."

"And you are right too, Olivia," Grandma said as she gave Olivia a "high five."

"Ohhh, fertile, ohhhh agriculture," Abby said. "Why can't you guys talk like me? Let's just say it's good farmin' up here!"

"And Abby, once again, you are right as well—it is good farmin' up here," Grandma laughed and gave Abby a high five.

Ask-a-cuz: Was there really a Lake Agassiz?

There sure was.

According to the encyclopedia.com, Lake Agassiz was a glacial lake of the Pleistocene epoch. That period lasted a couple of million years and ended about 11,000 years ago.

Lake Agassiz was formed about 14,000 years ago when the continental ice sheet melted. The lake covered much of northwestern Minnesota, northeastern North Dakota, and parts of Canada.

As the ice melted, the water drained east into Lake Superior and after the ice disappeared the water drained north into Hudson Bay.

The old bed of Lake Agassiz is the Red River Valley. Because of its rich soil, it is an important crop-growing area.

"So now that you know a bit about the history of this area, you can see why people could have traveled by boat into the heart of North America," Grandma said very seriously and looked around at her family sitting around her.

"Wait." Abby said. "How did you get so smart Grandma?"

"Abby!" Olivia said. "Grandma knows lots of things."

"Yeah," Added Lexi. "Grandma probably knows a lot of stuff—especially about history since she's been around for most of it."

"You girls are on a kick about my age today, aren't you," laughed Grandma. "Well, I used to teach 4th grade and we covered this information in social studies."

"Secondly, your grandpa studied this history and the legend of Viking travel in this area" she continued. "I have saved Grandpa's notes and items that he collected during his study and investigation of the Viking legends."

With a bit of pageantry, Grandma opened the crate and pulled out a 6 inch brown plastic statue of a rock.

"This is a replica of the Kensington Runestone," she explained. "Over 100 years ago, a farmer in Minnesota found the stone on his land. The writings on it indicate that Vikings were here in Minnesota in 1362—130 years before Christopher Columbus discovered America."

"Wooooow, Grandma, it's just like Olivia said," Abby whispered and she let out another slow, low whistle. "Is the Kensington Runestone a mooring stone too?"

"No, Abby, it's not a mooring stone that Vikings used to anchor the boats, but the Kensington Stone does tell the tale that Vikings traveled here by boat. Some historians think the Vikings traveled on a waterway from the Atlantic to right here in what is now Minnesota," Grandma explained with an excited glint in her 83-year-old blue eyes.

Grandma was happy to see interest from her grandkids in something that was important to Grandpa Jonsrud.

> **Ask-a-cuz:** Is there really a Kensington Runestone?
>
> There sure is.
>
> Olof Ohman and his son found the slab of stone with strange writing on it at their farm in 1898 near Kensington Minnesota.
>
> Hjalmer R. Holand, a University of Wisconsin graduate student translated the writing on the stone to read "8 Goths and 22 Norwegians on exploration journey from Vinland over the west. We camp by 2 skerries one day-journey from this stone. We were and fished one day. After we came home, 10 men red with blood and tortured. Hail Virgin Mary, save from evil. Have 10 men by the sea to look after our ship, 14 day - journeys from this island year 1362."
>
> Five scholars appointed by the Minnesota Historical society believed the Kensington Runestone to be real.
>
> The stone is 31 inches high, 16 inches wide, six inches thick and weighs 202 pounds.
>
> Read more about it from the writing of Vikings Researcher William. P. Holmen at http://kensingtonmn.com/runestonepg.html, or visit the Runestone Museum in Alexandria, Minnesota (https://www.runestonemuseum.org/).

You can draw! Draw Grandma and the cousins looking in the crate at the Kensington Runestone model.

Chapter 3: *Grandpa's search*

After everyone had a chance to look at the Kensington Runestone, Grandma Jonsrud continued her story.

"So this is all pretty exciting, but I have more to tell you," Grandma said.

She lowered her voice as if she was afraid someone else might hear her.

It was very quiet except for the wind and snow blowing against the cabin windows and jingle bells ringing in the distance.

"Grandpa also discovered some little known clues. Clues that could lead you to a real Viking discovery."

Now you could hear a pin drop in the living room of the Senior log cabin because the cousins and their parents were holding their breath and listening so intently.

Of course no one dropped a pin—that's just a saying.

But, still. If someone did drop a pin, you would gosh darn hear it.

Grandma pulled out an old piece of paper that had tracings on it. It looked similar to when you place a paper on an object and then scribble on the paper to transfer the markings from the object to the paper.

Lexi stood up to be close to her Grandma.

"Grandma, what is it," she asked.

"Well that's what I'm going to tell you about, Lexi," Grandma said.

Grandma smiled at her granddaughter and continued with her story. "In 1974, your Grandpa met with Ole Herbson, the old farmer who used to own the land that Junior is built on."

"One day Grandpa walked with Ole on one of Ole's fields. Ole showed Grandpa a stone that he found when he was plowing his field to plant corn," Grandma continued.

"The rock had strange writing on it. From your grandpa's studies—although he couldn't read it--he knew the writing was similar to the writing on the Kensington Runestone," she said.

"Wow," Lexi said.

"Because Grandpa didn't have a camera with him, he took an impression of writing on the rock using a paper and pencil," Grandma explained. "And this is it."

"Well, where is the stone," asked Lexi.

"Why didn't Grandpa go back and take a picture of it," asked Olivia.

"What do the markings say," asked Abby.

The cousins were a natural team in everything they did, including riddling their Grandma with questions.

"Well, slow down girls," Grandma laughed. "You make it tough on an old lady to tell a story!"

The cousins grinned and waited to hear more.

Grandma explained that Grandpa had gone back the next morning to the place where Ole had shown him the slab and he brought a camera to take a picture of it, but the slab had disappeared!

Grandpa searched the area and went to Ole's farmhouse to ask Ole what had happened. But for some reason Ole just said it was better left alone and refused to talk about it again.

Grandpa didn't understand Ole's strange behavior and he never did find the stone again.

"Trying to still figure out the mystery, Grandpa showed the tracing to a young, local historian named Otto Larsen at the Detroit Lakes Museum," Grandma said.

"Otto thought the words looked like ancient Nordic writing, but he was not able to read it, and without the actual stone, no one else took your Grandpa seriously. Dejected, Grandpa eventually put this paper in his box and stuck the box in our bedroom closet," Grandma said as she patted the crate.

Everyone was quiet for a moment thinking about how Grandpa must have felt.

Then Olivia broke the silence.

"So we don't know what this inscription says," she said as she stared at the partly crumpled, yellowed paper.

Suddenly, she sprang up and ran to the kitchen door, pausing only to jump into her boots before running outside to the cold and dark.

A few moments later, Olivia returned with snowflakes in her hair and a camera in her hand.

"I got my camera from the car! We need to take a picture of Grandpa's paper so that Lexi, Abby and I can pursue Grandpa's mystery, for Grandpa, for us, and for Vikings everywhere," she declared as she snapped a number of photos, carefully capturing the writings as best that she could.

"Okay, everyone," Lexi's Mom interrupted. "This is all extremely exciting, but we have to eat before it gets too late. This mystery has been around for at least 30 years—and who knows--maybe 1,000 years--so one more night won't make a difference. Now wash up for dinner."

With that, the Jonsrud clan sat down at the table and enjoyed hot soup, sandwiches, chocolate milk, and of course, Uncle Lyle's famous Christmas sugar cookies.

Then the cousins split up for the night—Lexi stayed with her parents and Grandma at the Senior cabin, and Olivia and Abby's family went back to the--by then--warm Junior cabin.

Chapter 4: *Duncan, donuts, Ole and julebukking*

Abby awoke to a sound that any kid in Minnesota loves in the winter. She heard a thud against the window above her bed, followed by what sounded like the brush of a snare drum.

Abby thought about the noise that way because she liked music and played both the piano and guitar.

Instantly, Abby grinned because she knew someone had just thrown a snowball at her window.

She looked up to see the remains of the snow ball sliding down the outside of the glass.

Since she and Olivia slept in built-in pine beds in the loft, it meant someone had a pretty good arm to hit their window two stories up.

She rubbed her eyes and looked at the pretty, glistening snow on the window. Bright sunshine streamed in through window.

What a great time the Christmas holiday was in Minnesota!

While the sunshine was bright and warm coming in through the window, Abby knew that it was probably very cold outside this far north of the equator in December. Still, she thought, the cold was nothing that her snowsuit couldn't handle.

She jumped out of bed and looked out the window to the wintry scene below.

There was a four foot blanket of brilliant white, sparkling snow everywhere. Their land looked like a Christmas card. It was a grand lawn surrounded by tall pine trees and leafless large oak and maple trees. To top it off, the morning sun shone brightly out of the brilliant blue sky.

In the middle of the yard, standing knee-deep in the snow was Lexi and her dad Monty.

They were grinning from ear to ear as they formed snowballs in their mittens to throw another round at Abby's window.

Grandma Jonsrud was there too, but she stood in the shoveled driveway to stay dry and out of the line of fire.

Abby waived and motioned them to come to Junior's front door.

Lexi throws a snowball at Abby.

You can draw! Draw Abby looking out the window at Lexi, Monty and Grandma below in the snow.

Abby turned to look back inside at her sleeping sister.

"Ohhh-liv-i-ahhhhhh!" Abby whispered loudly in her big sister's ear. "It's time to get up!"

Olivia was a slow riser in the morning because she spent her evenings thinking. She opened one eye, stared at Abby and let out a low, irritated whine.

"Abbyyyyy—leave me alone," Olivia said.

"Oh-liv-i-ahhhh--rememberrrrrrrr—we have a mystery to solve and to find Grandpa's Viking treasure," Abby said as she bounced on her sister.

The chance to solve a mystery—especially for a Grandpa whom she had never met was too good to ignore.

In one swift move, Olivia turned on her side--and like a bronco--bucked Abby off of her and on to the pine floor.

Abby was in too good of a mood to care that she had just tumbled to the floor. Giggling, she picked herself up and galloped down the stairs to welcome Lexi, Monty and Grandma. They were in the 4-season porch shedding their outdoor winter clothes.

"Good morning Grandma and Uncle Monty, do you want a cup of coffee," Abby asked. The cousins were very respectful of their elders.

"Well then Abby, get them a cup on the double," Lexi ordered excitedly. Hey the cousins were kids—they weren't always as respectful with each other!

"Grandma and Dad are going to take us to the Detroit Lakes museum to see Otto Larsen," Lexi continued. "Remember him? He was the expert that Grandpa showed the imprint of the slab to."

"Ohh, yes I dooo, duuude," Abby sang as she danced in circles to deliver sloshing cups of coffee to her Grandma and uncle.

Abby could dribble coffee almost better than she dribbled a basketball—and that was pretty good. But let's get real. Dribbling hot coffee is not good.

"Abby, be careful," her mom said.

Uncle Monty laughed and took a cup from Abby.

"That's okay, I'm excited too," he said. "Grandma's story kept me thinking most of the night and that's why I googled Otto to find that he still works at the Detroit Lakes Museum."

"Well, I'll have to work on my bedtime stories if they are keeping you all up at night," Grandma joked.

"No Grandma. Don't change a thing, it kept me thinking during the night too," Olivia said as she slung her hair into a pony tail and walked down the stairs from the loft.

"We've been looking for a new mystery. And Grandma, you and Grandpa—and Abby with her mooring stone--have given us a great mystery for this Christmas," Olivia said.

Abby held up her index finger and waived it to make a point.

"Ahhh--excuse me, 'candle holder'," she said with authority.

Abby's dad tousled her hair and said, "Yes, Abby, a mooring stone <u>and</u> a candle holder.

Everyone gobbled a quick breakfast of fruit, milk, toast and peanut butter. Then Jon and Beth waved good-bye and the cousins, Grandma, and Monty drove to the city of Detroit Lakes.

Soon the cousins were inside the 112-year-old Detroit Lakes museum. They saw a man near the front door and they asked him if he was Otto Larsen.

The man answered, "Nope, I'm Duncan. I work with Otto. How can we help you?"

Duncan dunked his chocolate-covered donut in a steaming cup of coffee and slurped it.

"We need to talk to Mr. Larsen about a Viking artifact that our Grandpa shared with him about 40 years ago," Olivia volunteered.

Duncan swallowed hard and wiped his mouth with his hand.

"So you're the Jonsruds who called this morning," Duncan said. "Ever since I started working here a year ago, old Otto has been talking about that darn rock with writing on it. And now because you called him this morning, he's jumping around the museum like the floor is a trampoline.

Olivia made a mental note that Duncan liked to stretch the truth a bit. She couldn't imagine anyone jumping very high on a marble floor—and jeesh--certainly not like it was a trampoline.

"Yes, we want to talk to Mr. Larsen and ask him to take another crack at translating the ancient Nordic writing," Lexi explained.

"Well, come on this way to the archive room," Duncan said and he went up the white marble steps two at a time.

The girls scampered up the steps behind Duncan and Grandma and Monty followed in close pursuit.

When Duncan opened the door to the archive room, they saw a man with white hair, a neatly trimmed beard, and wire-rimmed glasses, sitting at a table. He was reading under the light of a small desk lamp.

"Whoa, I thought Grandpa had talked to a young historian," Abby said to her sister and cousin. "Dudes, this guy is more history than historian."

"Abby! You are so rude," Olivia whispered and pinched her sister.

Duncan snickered. He took another bite of his donut and gulped his coffee.

Otto bent over and looked Abby straight in the eye. Abby saw the twinkle in his old blue eyes.

"Well, that's okay," said Otto. "The youngster has a point. It was almost 40 years ago when I talked to your Grandpa, and I was a lot younger then."

"The fact is, that I don't remember conversations from last week, let alone that long ago, except your Grandpa was so serious and the imprint he showed me was so real-looking. For years, I wished I had a copy of that imprint or at least your Grandpa's name so that I could contact him," Otto said.

"Then uffda! Out of the clear blue--Merry Christmas to me--you called this morning," Otto said as he looked at Lexi's dad.

"Well, here's a copy of the imprint Mr. Larsen," Olivia said. She handed Otto a large photograph.

"Yes, by golly, that's it," Otto said excitedly. "You know, since meeting your Grandpa 40 years ago, I studied ancient Nordic writings for just such a chance as you're giving me today to do it right this time."

Otto looked at the photo carefully.

To the excited girls, it seemed like Otto stared at the photo forever, but it was probably only a few minutes. Then he looked at them, Grandma and Monty for a moment and muttered, "Uffda."

"What is it Otto," Duncan asked with a hint of irritation in his voice, mostly because he had just dropped a hunk of his donut on the floor.

Otto didn't respond to Duncan. Otto just looked back at photo, and then back at the group again.

"By golly, I think a couple of these words say something about a Viking ship," he finally said.

The whole group took steps to get closer to Otto.

"Whooaa! A Viking ship? Are you kidding me dude," Abby said in disbelief.

Yah, yah, I really think it says that, but let me study this to be sure, okay," Otto said trying to contain his own excitement. "I will call you in a couple of hours."

He shuffled the family and Duncan out of the archive room and shut the door behind them.

The cousins were thrilled with the possibility of the message, but disappointed that Otto couldn't read the whole message immediately.

When they were back at Junior, Lexi suggested that the three of them go visit Ole Herbson's family to pass the time. Ole had passed away a few summers ago, but his son's family lived down the county road from Junior. By car, the Herbsons lived a couple of miles away, but by foot it was much closer.

The cousins set out from Junior into the snowy woods and cut through an old tractor path toward the Herbson farm.

"Look! There's the great palm tree Christmas tree in their yard that we can see shining through the woods at night every Christmas," Abby pointed out as they cut across the ditch and onto the long snowy, gravel driveway to the Herbson home.

"It's really not Christmas at Long Lake without seeing the Herbson's Christmas palm tree!"
Abby said with glee.

Olivia nodded but was more interested in thinking of questions to ask the family about the stone that Ole had shown Grandpa in the field so many years ago.

Lexi knocked on the door.

Very soon, a girl about the age of the cousins opened the door. She didn't look too startled to see a pack of Jonsruds on her doorstep. Perhaps it was because it was Christmas time and she thought her neighbors were beginning to "julebukk" for the holiday season.

Ask-a-cuz: What is julebukking?
The tradition of the Christmas buck—or julebukk--is said to have started in Norway over a thousand years ago in honor of the mythical god Thor and his goats. Today, julebukk is tied to Christmas instead of Thor. People still julebukk in the United States—usually in states with lots of people who are descendents from Norway and Sweden—such as Minnesota, North Dakota, South Dakota, and Wisconsin. In one version, people go from door to door singing Christmas songs. After they have sung, they are given candy or a drink, and then at least one person from that house joins the julebukkers to go to the next house.

"Are you julebukking," the girl asked. She was about to go get some candy to give the cousins and maybe join them in going to other houses along the frozen beach.

"No, but hi, I'm Olivia Jonsrud, and this is my sister Abby and my cousin Lexi," Olivia said. "That's our log cabin and our cousin's lake house on Uffda Vista Drive."

"And our Grandma's log cabin is on the opposite side of the lake—the one with the pine tree light with blue lights," Lexi added.

"Oh yeah, I know you guys, I run on Uffda Vista Drive—it's a great gravel road for training," the girl said. "I'm Jenny Herbson."

"Oh. Awesome. So guess what dude," Abby jumped into the conversation. "First, we really love your Christmas palm tree. And then, our Grandpa knew your Grandpa. And your Grandpa showed our Grandpa a rock with writing on it, but then we think your Grandpa hid it."

Abby took a big breath.

"What?" Jenny asked. Abby was a little too quick on telling the story.

"Now. There. You see Abby," Olivia said. "This is precisely why I suggest that you practice joke-telling. You skip right to the punch line and it confuses people."

"Oh-liv-i-ahhh, I'm just saying, you tell me to what to do way too often," Abby complained.

"So this is a joke, it's not julebukking," Jenny interrupted the sisters with a question.

"No, it's no joke and yes it's not julebuking. Abby is just excited--we all are," Lexi said. "Jenny, what we mean to say is that your Grandpa had a rock with special writing on it and we think it is still somewhere on your farmland. We'd like to find it."

"Jenny, we may be able to help the Jonsruds," said a voice from inside the Herbson house. "I wondered if a Jonsrud would ever show up asking about the rock."

Chapter 5: *A hideaway in clear sight*

Jenny turned around to look inside the house.

"What do you mean Dad," she asked.

Jenny's dad came to the door.

"You kids are talking about my dad. I remember a long time ago--I was about 6 years old when I helped Dad dig up a big slab from the field behind the woods at your place," Jenny's dad recalled.

"Dad told me we had to hide it because your Grandpa was so excited about the rock and seemed to think it was important," Jenny's dad continued.

"My dad wasn't sure if it was true. Your grandpa told him how a farmer that found that other Viking stone was hounded by history buffs and people accusing him of making it up," Jenny's dad continued with his story. "My dad didn't want to be a part of that. He thought if your Grandpa learned more about the rock that it would cause people to bug us, swarm our land and mess up Dad's fishing spots on the lake."

Olivia thought that her Grandpa would never let the lakes area be overrun with tourists and that he would have protected Ole Herbson.

From family stories, Olivia knew that Grandpa loved nature and the quiet beauty of the lakes area. But Olivia didn't say anything because she didn't want to break the spell that Jenny's dad seemed to be under.

"I had forgotten about it over the years, but it's kind of fun that you are asking about it now," Jenny's dad finished.

"Dad," Jenny started slowly to say, and then her eyes got bigger. "I think I know the rock that you are talking about!"

"Yah, I think you do Jenny," her dad said. "Go ahead now, show the girls."

Jenny pulled on her boots, coat, mittens and hat and jumped off the porch to the Herbson snow-covered front yard.

"Follow me girls," Jenny said as she high-stepped through the snow. She ran back toward the wooded area between the Herbson house and Junior.

Because the cousins had just tramped a path through the snow in that area, the four girls made good time even if it was a workout.

They were breathing hard and could see their breath in the cold air. Still, they didn't spot the breath of a man standing quietly in the woods watching them!

They ran until Jenny stopped at the old Herbson dumpsite. The dump had a mound of scrap metal and belongings of the Herbson family from times past.

"Oh no Jenny, we can't go into that heap. Our parents have told us to stay away from here because we could get hurt," Abby said as she stood back from the junk pile.

"And that's exactly why I bet my Dad and Grandpa put the rock near here," Jenny said. "But don't worry; we're not climbing into the junk heap."

She turned left and walked a few steps in the direction toward the cliff above the lake. Jenny stopped at a small hill, next to an old, big oak tree.

Jenny started digging in the snow.

Without being asked, the cousins dropped into the snow and started to dig too.

After they had created about a 2 foot by 2 foot clearing in the 3-foot deep snow, they could see an old green wooden door with rusty hinges and doorknob.

Here was a secret hideaway very close to Junior!

The cousins had never noticed it before because the snow covered it well in the winter, and in the summer, the area was overgrown with the woods and prairie grass.

"What is it," Lexi asked.

Lexi stared at the old door leading into the snowy hill.

"I believe it is what they used to call a bomb shelter," Olivia said. "After World War II, some people were scared of another war so they built bomb shelters that they could go into to hide from attacks. I don't think anyone ever really used them except as a storage space."

Jenny didn't know the cousins too well, but she was impressed with Olivia's knowledge.

"Olivia's right," Jenny said. "I bet you can guess what Grandpa and Dad stored in here."

Jenny pulled hard on the door and it creaked opened far enough for them to enter one by one.

"Hang on," Lexi said. "I think we need some light before going in."

Lexi pulled out a flashlight from her pocket. Abby and Olivia pulled out flashlights from their pockets too. The cousins were always ready to investigate.

Inside, they could see by the light of their flashlights that it was a framed small room with a dirt floor and walls. Otherwise it was vacant.

Because it was the dead of winter, there were no bugs to worry about and with the door shut so tight, there were no critters either. In fact, it was quite empty.

"So are we missing something," Abby asked and swung her flashlight up to shine in Jenny's face.

Before, Olivia could tell her sister that it was rude to shine a light in someone's face, Lexi let out a yelp.

"Take a look at your feet, Abby," Lexi said excitedly.

Looking down they could see that they were standing on the rock slab.

The Herbson's had made the slab into the entryway of an old bomb shelter!

The slab was too heavy and wedged in the frozen ground for the girls to lift, but they swept dirt and snow from the face of the rock to reveal the odd writing that they had seen on Grandpa's paper!

They gathered around the slab and Olivia pulled out here camera to take pictures.

Since daylight is a very short amount of time in Minnesota winters--especially around Christmas-- the sun was already beginning to set.

As Olivia was finishing taking photographs of the slab, a movement outside of the bomb shelter caught Lexi's eye. Lexi moved to the doorway and could see the figure of a man standing in the trees watching them.

When he saw that Lexi had noticed him, he began to run away.

"You guys, someone is out here!" Lexi yelled.

The cousins pointed their flashlights in the direction in which Lexi pointed.

They could see a man running through the snow and woods toward the county road!

Instinctively, the cousins and Jenny gave chase, but they could not catch the man because he had a pretty good head start.

They stopped chasing him once they made it to the clearing and watched him reach the county road where he ran toward the town of Vergas.

The girls were uneasy that someone had been watching them, and wondered what he had wanted.

They were now cold and it was dark.

They returned to the bomb shelter to close the door and then walked Jenny back home.

You can draw! Draw a picture of the cousins and Jenny digging in the snow to find a green wooden door in the hill.

"Wow Jenny! What a find," Lexi said when they reached the Herbson home. "Thank you for showing it to us."

Before leaving, the cousins told Jenny that Otto Larsen was translating the words, and that one phrase seemed to say something about a Viking ship. Jenny was excited by the news.

They said good-bye to their new friend, and agreed to be careful and to get back together soon to talk more about the mystery.

The cousins headed back through the snowy woods to Junior.

They ran up the steps to Junior and threw off their snow clothes and boots once inside the door.

Their timing was perfect--the cousins were always pretty lucky at Long Lake—because Jon and Beth were ready to serve them a hot dinner.

As they were eating and telling Jon and Beth about the slab and the stranger that watched them, Beth's cell phone rang. It was Monty. He said that Otto had finished translating the writing.

Olivia and Abby were so excited that they didn't even remind their mom this time that if they had their own cell phone Monty could have called them directly.

Jon and Beth drove the cousins back to the museum where Grandma, and Lexi's parents, Monty and Connie joined them.

Soon they were all back in the museum's archive room with Otto.

"So we need to have other language experts verify what I am translating, but what I'm reading is the most exciting news around here in a long, long, l-o-n-g time," Otto said excitedly.

"Well, what does it say Mr. Larsen, what does it say," Abby asked. She couldn't stand still she was so excited. She was dancing around as if she was defending her basket in a basketball game.

Although Otto was too old to dance like Abby, it was clear that he was just as excited because he kicked one leg up and pumped his fist with a swing from his elbow.

"Otto, I have never seen you this animated, "Duncan said.

"You betchya, Duncan, this is the type of discovery that you yourself have dreamed of. It's the kind of stuff that makes you famous."

"And rich," Duncan asked. He reached for a donut from his desk and pulled up a chair to listen and watch.

Otto turned on a projector. Immediately, they could see a copy of the photo of the slab with circles around the ancient words and to the right of it, Otto's handwritten translation.

"Near as I can figure, it says—'30 Norwegians on journey from Vinland fishing in storm. No men drowned but we lost our ship. We camp to wait for second ship on exploration journey year 1362'," Otto said his voice trembling with excitement.

"Oh my gosh," Lexi said.

"We have a sunken ship," squealed Abby.

"This is really exciting," said Grandma with a big smile and glistening eyes. "I wish your Grandpa was right here right now—he'd be so happy."

"Oh Grandma, I think he is here in spirit," Lexi said with big eyes and a big smile.

"Since the rock was found at the top of our cliff," Olivia mused. "And we know that the lake levels were much higher hundreds of years ago..."

"And much of Minnesota and North Dakota was under water at one time," Lexi added.

"Could the sunken Viking ship be in Long Lake," Abby asked excitedly.

"And could the ship still be here after so many hundreds of years," Olivia finished with a second question.

The cousins had listened to Grandma's history lesson and were applying what they had learned.

Monty stroked his blonde and grey beard—a full-blooded Norwegian, he kind of looked like a Viking--as he thought about the girls' questions.

"Well. You know Olivia, 'yes' is a possible answer for both of your questions," Monty said slowly.

Monty always talked slowly when he thought about stuff.

"If the ship's wood prettified—turned to stone—it would still be here," he said.

How could that be, Uncle Monty," Abby asked.

"Well Abby, wood can petrify over long periods of time when it is soaked in water that contains minerals," Monty explained. "And Long Lake certainly has minerals in it. If a Viking ship went down in 1362, it has had 1,000 years to petrify."

"And that's plenty of time," he said. "Think about it. It only takes two days for your Mom's meatloaf to turn as hard as stone. Heh heh."

Monty chuckled at this own joke.

Connie rolled her eyes for Monty making a joke about her meat loaf and at such an important time.

"Norwegian humor," she said shaking her head.

Ask-a-cuz: How does wood petrify?

According to "How Stuff Works" at http://science.howstuffworks.com/environmental/earth/geology/petrified-wood-info.htm, wood petrifies when it soaks over a long period of time, in water containing minerals. Over time, the mineral either fills every cavity of the wood or the mineral-containing water dissolves the wood and replaces it with mineral matter. The mineral forms a perfect copy of the original substance.

The rate of petrifaction is not exactly known. In some cases it may be fairly rapid.

"Did you knowwwwww—that my mooring stone may have been used by those same Vikings," Abby said, jumping up and down.

"How are we going to find that ship if it is in Long Lake," Olivia thought out loud as she absent-mindedly pulled on Abby's shirt to slow down Abby's jumps.

"Ho-ho-ho! I think I may be able to help you guys," said a familiar voice coming in to the archive room.

"Uncle Terry!" the cousins said in unison.

Uncle Terry and Aunt Angie had wandered into the room. No one had noticed their arrival because of all the excitement.

When Angie and Terry drove to Senior that night, they found Grandma's note explaining she had gone to the museum and why. So they drove into town to join the excitement.

"But wouldn't it be covered up with silt and sand over so many years," asked Olivia.

"Well your thinking is on track Olivia, but it could depend on the currents in the water and where the ship came to rest," Monty answered.

"You mean if it was on a cliff where the lake drops to lower levels, the ship could still be visible," said Lexi's oldest sister Brianne.

Brianne and Tricia, Lexi's big sisters had now also arrived at Senior for the holidays at Long Lake and found their way to the museum.

Brianne, Tricia and Monty were certified scuba divers and knew quite a bit about lake currents and the topography of the local lakes.

"If you really think there is a Viking ship somewhere on the bottom of Long Lake, then I think we need to do some ice fishing and use my new depth finder that your Aunt Angie just got me for Christmas," Uncle Terry said in a booming voice. "We can see lots of stuff down there in addition to fish."

"And we can start our search by using our depth maps of the lake," Tricia added.

Because Tricia, Brianne and Monty were scuba divers, they had depth maps of a few of the 10,000 lakes in Minnesota—including Long Lake.

As exciting as it all was, it was getting late and the lakes area forecast called for snow and blowing snow, so the group decided to head back to the Jonsrud cabins for the night.

They told Otto they would keep him up to date on their plans and actions.

Otto said he would contact some other language experts to get more opinions, but with it being the holiday, he didn't expect to make much more progress for a few days.

Jon, Beth, Olivia and Abby drove back to Junior. Grandma, Connie, Monty, their girls and Angie and Terry drove to Senior.

As big a group as that was, it was just beginning. The rest of the Jonsrud families would arrive the next day on Christmas Eve.

All were there, except Uncle Lyle and Aunt Skunk and their two daughters, Dani and Cali. They were arriving that night at their own lake house next to Junior.

By the way, Aunt Skunk's real name was Monica—the family had called her Skunk since she was two.

She was much older than that now.

But don't worry—the nickname Skunk didn't mean that Monica smelled or that her hair was black and white.

She smelled of nice perfume and she colored her hair.

Chapter 6: *Fishin' on Christmas Eve*

"Hey Mom, can I use your phone to call Brianne," Olivia asked Beth as soon as they got in the door at Junior. "And by the way..."

"Here's the phone Olivia and no you can't have your own cell phone yet," Beth answered in the middle of Olivia's sentence.

"Ha Duuude—she cut you off! We're going to have to try a new approach if we want our phone," Abby laughed as she fed Dakota his dinner.

"Olivia, I always say, it's like going in for a layup," Abby continued. "If someone is blocking your path to the basket, all you do is fake a move toward that path, and then spin and go another route. That's all I'm saying Olivia."

"I knooooww, Abby, I knooow," Olivia muttered.

But Olivia didn't say more.

She had forgotten about the cell phone and was focused on learning more from Brianne about the lake map. She also wanted to set a plan with Uncle Terry to get out on the lake as early as possible the morning of Christmas Eve.

"Hi Olivia. Yes, we're looking at the map right now," Brianne said over the phone. "There are definitely a half dozen spots that look interesting right off the bat because of the depth of the lake as well as the currents within the lake."

> **Ask-a-cuz:** What causes currents in lakes?
>
> According to Yahoo's Ask at
> http://answers.yahoo.com/question/index?qid=20090709084217AAOqoDt
>
> There are a number of causes for currents or water flow in lakes, including wind across the top, the density of water, inflow and outflow from the lake, and even obstacles and hills and valleys on the lake bottom.

"And girls, get some sleep tonight as we will head out to the lake tomorrow morning as soon as the sun is up," yelled Uncle Terry into Brianne's phone.

They all hung up.

What a night.

Not only was it the eve before Christmas Eve at the Senior and Junior cabins, it was also the night before the cousins began looking for a Viking ship that may have sunk in their very own lake a thousand years ago.

Everyone was excited, but needed to calm down and go to sleep for the night.

That night, Abby and Olivia lay in their beds looking at the muted glow of red, green, and blue lights reflecting on the cabin pine ceiling from their Christmas tree below on the main floor.

They could hear the old Christmas tunes playing softly.

Olivia imagined how the ship might look at the dark bottom of Long Lake.

Olivia imagined how the ship might look at the dark bottom of Long Lake.

"Oh-liv-i-ahhhh," Abby whispered, breaking into Olivia's visions of a Viking ship. "Do you think Santa delivered presents to the Vikings?"

"I do not know for sure, Abby, but I bet that he did,' Olivia yawned and answered her little sister.

"Girls—no more talking," their dad Jon called from the main floor. "And girls?"

"Yes, Dad," the sisters answered together.

"Merry Christmas!"

"Woo-hoo," yelled Abby.

"Yeaahhh," yelled Olivia.

"Jon! Don't get them riled up—they need to go to sleep," Beth said.

The girls laughed and they could hear their parents laughing too.

It had been a long day at Long Lake. But it wasn't long before the girls were fast asleep with visions of sugar plums and Viking ship bows dancing in their heads.

About eight hours later, before Abby opened her eyes, she had that wonderful feeling—the kind you get when you know it is the beginning of a very special day.

It was Christmas Eve and they were hunting sunken Viking ships!

Abby kicked off her blankets, and pretending she was a ninja warrior, she rolled off her bed, landed on her feet on the floor-- and with one big jump--pounced on Olivia still sleeping in her bed.

Abby didn't quite finish her "Ohhh-liv-i-ahhhhhh—Meeerrrrry Christmas!" because Olivia was so startled that she instinctively kicked Abby off of her and on to the floor.

"Olivia, I'm just sayin' you are a flirting with being more naughty than nice on the most important day of my year," Abby said as she brushed herself off and stood up. "That's all I'm sayin'."

"Someday, Abbyyyyy—to the moon," Olivia said and she climbed out of bed. "Anyway, you are right Merry Christmas and a happy sunken Viking ship."

The girls gave each other a high five and then raced down the stairs.

 Their mom, dad and Dakota were already up and having coffee. Actually, Dakota was chewing on a bone--their parents were the ones drinking coffee. Dakota ran around fast enough all day. He certainly didn't need any coffee.

The sisters sat at the counter and ate their bananas and French toast sticks as quickly as they could.

They dressed in their full winter suits because it was cold out on the lake, and there was nothing to break the cold wind until they went inside Terry's fish house.

As the Jonsruds were getting ready to leave, Jenny came running up their long, snow-covered, gravel driveway.

"Hey are you julebukking," Abby joked.

"I was jogging so maybe we can call it jule-jogging," Jenny laughed. "Do you have some candy for me?"

"Well, I think I do," Beth said and gave Jenny a piece of homemade fudge.

Jenny thanked Beth for the treat and then Jenny and the sisters agreed they would call each other if they found anything today.

The Jonsruds climbed into their car and headed to the Senior cabin.

Lexi was at the top of the hill when the Jonsruds arrived at Senior. Running alongside the car, Lexi raced them down the long slippery driveway.

When she fell about half way down, she found that sliding was almost as quick and more fun. She giggled, rolled and slid to a stop next to Jonsrud's parked car.

Olivia and Abby climbed out of the car and the trio of cousins jumped and slid around in excitement.

While Grandma sipped on her coffee and watched from the warmth of Senior, Monty and Connie, and Angie and Terry worked outside and hooked up a sled to each of the two snowmobiles by Senior's doorstep. They had loaded up one sled with the gear and food they would need for a day on the lake.

"Girls, take my cell phone, but keep it in your inside zippered pocket," Beth said to Abby and Olivia.

"Yeah, even if it is waterproof, we don't want that phone to end up on the deck of the Viking ship at the bottom of the lake," their dad joked. "No one would believe that Vikings had cell phones."

Olivia couldn't help herself. She answered, "Well, it's just as difficult to believe that Abby and I are two of only the three kids on our school bus that don't have--."

Abby threw an elbow into Olivia's side and cut off Olivia's response.

"Olivia, remember the naughty and nice list," hissed Abby.

"Especially, to-daaay," Lexi muttered out of the side of her mouth.

"Okay girls, let's get crackin'," Uncle Terry said. Then he let out a loud laugh.

"And I do mean cracking—that ice is about two feet thick and we're going to have to crack through it. But that ice is no match for my augerrrrrrrrr arrr arrrrrh." Uncle Terry sounded like a growling bear.

The girls grinned at their uncle. Aunt Angie just shook her head.

"We're going to try over there first," Monty said, pointing to the left which was in the northwest direction of the lake. "Are you girls ready to climb in the toboggan?"

Monty didn't have to ask twice. Led by Lexi, the cousins jumped headfirst into the open sled.

Monty handed Lexi a waterproof tube. She slung it over her shoulder so that it would be secured tightly during the fun and wild ride to their first spot where they would look for the ship, and of course fish for Uncle Terry.

The tube that Lexi carried contained the map that her big sisters and dad had created the night before. Monty would show them how to read it because Brianne and Tricia weren't going ice fishing--they had to do some last minute Christmas shopping.

Soon Terry's and Monty's snowmobiles were roaring across Senior's snowy front yard toward the lake.

With all the snow, the ride for the girls was very smooth although the girls needed their face masks to keep their skin safe from the bitter cold.

The sun was shining brightly coming up on the east side, so the snow flying through the air sparkled like nature's Christmas present to the world. It was a wonderful Christmas Eve.

Olivia looked around as their sled cut across the lake. There were a number of fishing houses on the lake.

The fishing houses reminded Olivia of miniature Charles Dickens's Christmas villages that people put on their mantles to remember days gone by. But these fishing houses were big and real.

Besides the Jonsrud sleds, only two other snowmobiles and one small blue pickup truck were running on the lake this morning. Olivia noticed the truck because it was moving slowly in the distance behind them.

What if the truck was following them, she thought.

Her attention to the truck was broken because just then the cousins' sled hit a big pile of snow that sent each of the girls flying about a foot in the air. They all came down in a pile, still safely inside the sled.

Monty and Terry stopped the snowmobiles to make sure the girls were okay.

The trio of giggles coming from the big, white smiles in the opening in the girls' facemasks told Monty and Terry that they had nothing to worry about, and they started again toward their first spot.

Although it looked like the rest of the snowy, icy surface of the lake, Terry and Monty knew where to stop because they had come out earlier, dropping off Terry's new red wooden fish house. They had planted it where they thought it was the deepest point on Long Lake—128 feet deep.

Over the years, Olivia had wondered where the 128 foot spot was—now she, Lexi and Abby would get a chance to check it out.

You can draw! Draw the cousins being pulled in a sled behind a snowmobile across the frozen lake.

Terry and Monty and the girls worked as a team to prepare the site. Monty pulled the auger off the sled and placed it near the fish house.

Terry unlocked the fish house and the girls brought in the food, flashlights, and Terry's tackle box and placed it on the built-in bench.

Terry was the "king" of fishermen in the Jonsrud family and all of the ice fishing equipment belonged to him. He normally used his portable fishing house which was lighter and easier to move around on the ice. But today he and Monty had brought out Terry's new big fishing house.

"The bigger, wooden house goes well with my new state of the art, sonar depth-finder," Terry explained. "Besides, the weather forecast calls for snow and wind in the afternoon. This baby will hold all of us and keep us really warm." He lovingly patted his fishing house.

While Terry didn't fully believe that they were looking for a real sunken Viking ship, he was as excited as the girls to try out his new equipment and to catch a few fish along the way.

"Well, girls you know the drill, right," Terry asked. And then he laughed at his own play on words. "You know, you know the drill—you know the process we'll follow, and you know the drill—you know, this auger!"

Terry laughed so hard that the girls and Monty laughed too.

"Okay, so girls pick a spot that you like for where we will drill our first hole of the day for the hol-i-day," Terry laughed again. "Oh, I am so funny!"

"Uncle Terry," Abby groaned but pointed to a spot.

Terry picked up the auger and carried it to the spot to where Abby pointed.

Twice, he pulled hard on the cord of the auger. The auger roared to life. He put the tip on the ice and the auger started to drill into the ice.

In a matter of moments, a gush of pretty blue-green water shot up through the hole and it almost looked like Terry had struck oil. The water quickly turned to more ice on top of ice and snow.

Uncle Terry drills a fishing hole with his auger.

After that, Terry drilled two more holes in a line. Then the girls helped him and Monty push the fish house over the holes.

Within minutes, they group was inside the fish house and setting up their chairs around the holes.

"Wait a minute!" Lexi said. "This isn't quite right yet."

She pulled out two strings of Christmas lights—one set for inside the house and one set for outside of the house.

Olivia and Abby clapped and helped her string lights. The three cousins sang Christmas carols and Terry plugged in the cords to his generator. It was now a festive looking fishing house.

"Okay," Lexi said. "Now we can begin Uncle Terry."

The cousins each had their own fishing pole and knew how to use it so that their lines didn't freeze to the edge of the fishing holes or tangle with the other lines. In addition, they took turns using the scooper to skim the thin layers of ice that continually formed in the hole.

Normally, the girls would have plopped into place with their fishing gear. But today they were not interested in dropping their fishing lines in the holes.

They watched as Terry dropped the sonar line down the middle hole into the deep water below.

They could see the line for a few feet deep into the water, but then the line quickly disappeared into the first light green, then dark blue-grey water.

"Girls, we have a long way to go with the line. It's 128 feet deep here," Terry explained. "Still with my new equipment we will be able to see the bottom of the lake quite clearly."

Terry pointed out images on the monitor and explained how to understand what they were seeing.

In a few moments, they could see that the line had reached the floor of the lake.

"This is soooo exciting," Olivia said.

"What's that," Abby asked and pointed to two different images on the screen.

"Well, the first looks like an old tree log," Terry answered. "See how it's laying on the bottom of the lake?"

"And the second spot here is a school of fish," he continued. The girls could see the fish moving on the screen.

For the next 15 minutes, they surveyed the lake floor area and learned how to read the sonar screen and use the equipment.

As exciting as it was, they did not find anything that resembled a Viking ship. Over the next four hours, using Brianne and Tricia's diving map, they repeated their process in different areas of the lake.

The group had lunch about 1 p.m. And they caught and released a few fish along with their ship hunting.

As the hours passed and it grew closer to the evening—or the eve of Christmas--Olivia noticed that the other snowmobiles and fisherman had left the ice. All accept the blue truck. She had a sense that something wasn't right with that truck, but she also had a feeling what was going to be said next.

Chapter 7: *Surprise, surprise*

"Girls, we're going to have to wrap it up pretty soon," Monty said as he looked at the sun low in the sky and clouds rolling in from the west.

"Ahh Dad," Lexi said.

"How about just checking one more spot," Abby pleaded.

"Yes, Uncle Monty, how about if we just try a spot that is in front of Junior and Senior," Olivia reasoned. "It's kind of on our way back anyway."

Terry and Monty looked at each other and then nodded.

"Sure, why not," said Terry. "Just consider it your Christmas present from me." And he laughed really hard again at his own joke.

They gathered their equipment and moved to a spot about 100 yards out on the lake from the shore of Junior. At that spot, the map showed that the lake was about 100 feet deep.

They had just finished setting up for their final search of the day, when Monty's phone rang and he answered it.

"Oh my gosh! You're kidding me. No, I'll be right there," Monty said into the phone. "I'll get over there right away and then come back and help Terry shut down the fish house for the night."

Monty got off the phone and hurriedly told Terry and the girls that Tricia had fallen while ice skating on the lake in front of Senior.

Tricia had a nasty bump on her head and may have broken her wrist. They needed Monty's medical card to take her to the hospital.

"Monty, just go. I can shut down our fishing hole in three little trips," Terry said. "Don't worry. Just get Tricia into the doctor before the snow comes in and you guys get stranded."

Monty took a snow mobile and sled, and headed back to Senior. Terry began loading up the second sled with all the outdoor equipment first.

"Girls, by the looks of the weather, we can't wait for Monty to return and help us load up. I'm going to start with a load now," Terry said when he came inside the fish house. "You can take your final hunt for the Viking ship. I'll be back in a few minutes to lock up and bring you back to Senior. Just stay inside the fish house and stay warm. We're about to get a storm I think."

"We'll be fine Uncle Terry," Lexi reassured him.

"Yes, we have important work here to do," Olivia said as she plugged in the equipment again.

Olivia and Lexi were beginning to settle into their seats by the hole so that they could turn on sonar equipment and adjust the monitor.

Abby had tired of that work. She was shooting a nerf ball at a basket hoop set up in the corner of the fish house.

Terry looked outside. The wind had come up pretty strongly, and the snow was falling. He looked back inside the fish house. The girls looked happy, safe, and warm.

"Okay then. Be sure and lock the door girls," he said as he shut the door and headed to his snowmobile.

"Ah huh," Abby answered absent-mindedly as she sunk a mighty hook shot from across the fish house. "Oh ye-ah, oh ye-ah, oh ye-ah," Abby chanted and she executed a victory dance that looked better than some end-zone NFL victory dances.

With her celebration though, she forgot to lock the door behind Terry as he had instructed.

Abby continued playing basketball and Olivia and Lexi concentrated on surveying the new area of the lake floor. The wind howled outside, but the girls didn't notice--they were warm and having fun.

About 20 minutes later, Olivia looked at the clock on her mom's phone. She wondered what was keeping Terry from returning.

Looking out the small window, she finally noticed the blowing snow. It was looking pretty bad out there.

"We better call and see what's taking Terry so long," Olivia said. Before she could dial, the phone rang in her hands. It was her dad Jon.

"Olivia, Terry is here and we have three snowmobiles ready to go, but we're waiting until this wind dies down," Jon said. "We can't see anything at the moment—it's a serious blizzard.

"But don't get nervous. We'll be there as soon as we can. You girls just stay put and we'll be there soon," Jon continued.

Olivia could hear the nervousness in her dad's voice. She knew they were in a dangerous situation but that they would be fine if they just stayed in the safety of the fishing house.

"Okay, Dad—we're fine. Don't worry about us. We'll see you a bit," Olivia said and hung up the phone. "And Dad—how is Tricia?"

"Oh yeah, Tricia is doing okay—her wrist is just sprained and she's resting," Jon answered.

Olivia was glad to hear that her cousin was going to be alright. She hung up the phone, but didn't have a chance to relay her dad's message to Lexi and Abby because Lexi jumped up from her seat.

"Whooooah, what is that," Lexi said as she looked at the monitor.

Olivia moved closer to the screen to see what Lexi was pointing at.

"Lexi, I think it's just a ledge—you know—I think we're seeing where the lake floor is dropping from 90 feet or so to something deeper," Olivia said as she studied the screen.

"No, not that," Lexi said excitedly as she pulled off her mitten to point directly to a shape at the corner of the display.

This!"

"Oh," Olivia gasped. "Holy crap!"

"Oh-liv-i-ahhh! Remember the naughty and nice list tonight! You are getting close to saying some of those words we're not supposed to say," Abby said as she reached behind the built-in bench to grab her nerf ball.

"Holy crap!" Lexi repeated.

"Jeesh, you guys are messin' with Santa, that's all I'm sayin'" Abby muttered.

Then Abby chuckled.

"And how about saying 'holy carp'? It's more appropriate in the fish house and we don't tick off Santa," she said, clearly pleased with her creative solution.

But Olivia and Lexi didn't laugh.

Abby could see they were not kidding. She moved to the screen to see what her sister and cousin were looking at.

When she saw what they were looking at, she dropped the nerf basketball.

Abby wasn't sure, but the image on the sonar monitor looked like the front end of a big boat!

"Duuuudes," she said, "Holy carp!"

This time she didn't laugh either.

Abby, Lexi, and Olivia study the monitor to see what appears to be a sunken ship.

"Can you wiggle the line a bit to move it in that direction," Lexi directed Olivia.

Because of Terry's coaching throughout the day, Olivia had learned how to move the line within the confines of the small hole in the ice.

By moving her wrist in a circular motion, the line began to gyrate and the motion transferred from the top of the line to down the line in greater circles in the water until it moved the end of the sonar camera at the bottom a few feet in different directions.

Soon, Olivia was able to capture more of the image 90 feet below in the water.

It was a boat—a ship at the bottom of Long Lake!

All three of them squealed and jumped up and down, but then they sat down to look again in awe at what they had found.

"Wow! It has the shape of that Viking ship sitting in Moorhead in that museum," Lexi said.

Ask-a-cuz: Is there really a Viking ship in Moorhead?

There sure is.

The Hjemkomst Viking Ship is displayed in a museum in Moorhead, Minnesota. It was built by Robert Asp and his family, in Hawley, Minnesota beginning in 1973. The author of this book—Judi Stoa walked on the deck of the ship as it was being built. Judi's dad—a history buff—took his kids to see it in the mid 1970s because he understood that they were seeing history in the making.

The word "Hjemkomst" is Norwegian for "homecoming."

In 1982, Robert Asp's family sailed the ship to Norway to help prove that it was done by the Vikings many, many years ago.

To learn more about it, visit the Heritage Hjemkomst Interpretative Center at 202 first Avenue North in Moorhead. And tell them Judi and her dad sent you.

Or read more now by going to these websites:
http://www.hcscconline.org/secondarypages/hjemkomstship.html

http://www.hjemkomstcenter.com/

"The Moorhead ship is a replica of a real Viking ship that someone discovered about 100 years ago—and that ship is about 1,000 years old," Lexi said with glee.

"Oh my gosh," Abby said. "No one's going to believe us."

Even though she was staring at the distinct shape on the sonar monitor, Abby was having trouble believing what she was seeing.

"I believe you," said a man's voice as he opened the fish house door. The girls recognized the man!

"Hey, you're Duncan, Otto's assistant at the Detroit Lakes Museum," Olivia gasped.

"Yeah, right, assistant—I should be the director," scoffed Duncan.

"Whatever," Abby said, dismissing his comment.

Like her sister and cousin, Abby was alarmed that Duncan had abruptly entered their fish house.

"What are you doing here, dude?" she asked.

"I think I know, Abby," Olivia said.

"My guess is that Duncan has been a lot of places that we've been this week as we've worked on our mystery," Olivia said as she eyed Duncan closely.

"In fact, I think he's the man that we chased through the woods from the bomb shelter," she said.

"And I think that he probably drives a blue pickup truck and that his truck is parked outside now," Olivia added.

"Well, the kid is right," Duncan said to the girls. He looked at Olivia.

"You are pretty smart, aren't you," he said. "But I've known that since I met the three of you at my museum this week."

"Duuuude. It's not your museum. You are not the director—Otto is," Abby corrected him.

"Yeah, yeah kid. I know! I'm not the director, but I should be," Duncan said, looking at Abby. "I moved here a year ago because the Chicago Museum fired me. But after today, no one will call me assistant again or fire me again. I'm going to be famous for discovering a sunken Viking ship."

"Hey, wait a minute, you've got that wrong, Dun-," Lexi said.

But Duncan interrupted before Lexi could finish her sentence.

"Listen up. Between you, me and the fish house, I owe it to you girls. When you showed up yesterday with your Nordic inscription, I thought Merry Christmas to me—this is the kind of discovery that I've been dreaming of for 10 years."

"And I gotta say, your work to solve this mystery over the last couple of days has been better than the work of historians for a hundred years," Duncan continued. "I feel a little bad that you're not going to get credit for it, but I really need this discovery to advance my career."

"Hang on dude," Abby said exasperatedly.

She was using the word "dude" more and more as she got riled up by Duncan.

"We just found this sunken ship, not you and you cannot take credit for it," she said.

Abby stood to face Duncan. She put her hands on her hips for emphasis. Her hands and knees were shaking because she was scared, but she didn't want him to know that.

The smile on Duncan's face showed he was impressed by Abby's spunk.

"That's where you are wrong, squirt. Because I'm going to move your fish house away and then I'm going to tell the world I found that ship right below us," he explained. "I will tell everyone that I learned about that slab from you at the museum, but that's where the story will change. I'm going stay that I figured this whole thing out before you did."

"And as a bonus--any treasure on that ship will be mine. I could use the dough," Duncan finished with a laugh.

The girls hadn't even thought about treasure on board the ship.

Lexi's mouth dropped open in shock. In a protective move, she stood up to stand beside her cousin and to face Duncan.

Lexi also hoped that if they could keep Duncan talking maybe her dad and uncles would show up.

While Abby and Lexi confronted Duncan, Olivia remained seated behind them. Quietly she pulled out her mom's cell phone.

"So we'll just tell our family that you moved the fish house," Lexi said defiantly.

"Yeah, and it will be your word—a bunch of kids--against my word—me—a historian educated in this area," he laughed.

"And I'll be the one sitting on top of the ship. You ever hear of the phrase, 'possession is 9/10s of the law' kid?"

Lexi nodded yes.

"Well, I say that position is 9/10s of the law. And I'll be in a position that is closer to that ship than you. Get it," Duncan bragged and laughed.

The phone in Olivia's hand beeped as she dialed 9.

Before she could dial 1-1, Duncan heard the first beep and he looked directly at Olivia.

"Hey! What are you doing? Give me that phone," he demanded.

Olivia was scared. She tried to give herself some time to think.

So she stood up slowly and reached out to give him the phone. But then she too began feeling defiant.

She looked Duncan straight in the eye and then she deliberately let the phone drop out of her outreached hand—right down into the ice hole.

Splash!

Duncan jumped forward toward the hole, but he was too slow. He and the girls watched Beth's phone disappear as it sank quickly into the dark water below.

At first Duncan was mad as he looked up at Olivia, but then he began to smile.

"Well, that's fine, that's just fine," he said. "I guess you took care of it for me."

Duncan laughed stiffly.

"Okay, now all three of ya, let's get outside--you're going to help me cover up your tracks. Let's go!" he ordered.

The girls zipped up their jackets and pulled on their caps and mittens. It was hard to open the door because the wind was blowing so hard against it. They went walked out into the blizzard.

Seeing how bad it was outside, the three girls were sad because they understood that Duncan was right. Their tracks would be covered up and the fish hole would freeze over quickly in the brutal cold. There would be no evidence to prove that they were the ones that found the ship underneath the ice.

Duncan chained up the Jonsrud fish house to his truck. He made the girls climb into the cab of the truck and then he climbed in.

He dragged the house over a couple of feet and then jumped out to hammer a buoy into the ice by the girls' fishing hole.

Of course. The buoy had his name on it.

Duncan climbed back into the truck and started slowly driving northeast on the ice with the Jonsrud fish house in tow.

About a half mile later he stopped the truck. It was far enough away from the ship, but close enough so that the kids' family wouldn't notice--and couldn't prove--the change in location.

He unchained the fish house, climbed back into his truck and then called the Sheriff's office.

"Yeah, I want to report that I've discovered a sunken ship—maybe a Viking ship--here on Long Lake at Vergas," he told Sheriff Carly over the phone.

"Sure—yeah, I know it's a blizzard and Christmas Eve, but when you find something as important as this, Sheriff, you gotta report it, you know," Duncan said.

He grinned and winked at the girls, but then he shook his fist as a warning to the cousins to keep quiet while he was on the phone.

"Sure—I can meet you out here tomorrow," he said. "I have it marked with a buoy so I don't lose my spot or my claim."

Duncan hung up from the sheriff and then dialed the museum. He knew it was closed, but he wanted to leave a message on the recorder for Otto to report that he had found the ship.

Since the girls hadn't told anyone yet, Duncan was leaving a trail of messages with his calls that could later become a part of an official report. Duncan was a not-so-nice man, but he was pretty smart.

When he hung up, he turned and looked at the cousins once more.

"Okay now. You girls go back inside your fish house and you stay put--you hear me," he said. "It's warm and safe in there. Wait for your parents and you'll be okay."

Duncan was a bad enough guy to steal the credit for the discovery, but it appeared he wasn't a bad enough guy to let the girls be harmed in the blizzard.

Dejected, the girls climbed out of Duncan's truck and walked back to their fish house. As they opened their door, they turned to watch Duncan's truck disappear into the snowy night.

Once again safe inside their fish house, the three looked at each other and felt defeated.

"Too bad Duncan had a cell phone and we didn't," Abby moaned.

"Yeah, it could have been us who called in the reports," Lexi agreed.

"I know. This is just another dang reason that we should have a cell phone," Abby complained. "Do you realize we've been defeated by a cell phone?"

"Yes, can you believe it," Olivia said. "I don't really believe it, how will anyone else?"

"Well, our family will believe us," Lexi said. "That's worth something."

"It's not worth what that ship is worth," Abby responded wryly.

The cousins sat quietly and thought about the ship. They had gone through a big swing of emotions in a short amount of time--from being so excited to being so sad.

With nothing else to do, they watched through their small window and listened to the blizzard roaring outside.

After about 30 minutes, the weather started getting a little better. It wasn't long after that they heard the whirr of snowmobiles in the distance.

"Hey I think our dads are coming," Lexi said and she tried to see in the distance.

"Well, it's better late than never I guess," Abby said dejectedly.

Soon they saw Jon, Terry, and Monty drive up on three snowmobiles. The men brought three snowmobiles to get the girls off the ice once and for all for the night.

Inside the fish house, the girls excitedly told their dads and uncle the story of what had happened.

"Whoa, whoa, whoa," Jon said. "That's a big story. We believe you, but we have to get you home now."

"Jon's right," Monty said. "We need to get you in a warm house and get you something to eat."

"Yeah, we'll figure out what to do later," Terry added and he ruffled Abby's hair.

The six of them climbed on the snowmobiles and drove over the drifts of snow toward Senior.

It was a long drive back and even though this time the girls wore helmets and goggles to protect them from the brutal cold, each of them huddled behind their driver to try to stay out of the wind and stinging snow.

Finally, the three snowmobiles drove up from the ice and on to the snow drifts in Senior's yard. Jon, Monty and Terry pulled up as close as they could to the cabin, and the six Jonsruds stiffly climbed off the snowmobiles and trudged up the stairs to the front door.

They opened the door and entered the bright and warm cabin. Exhausted they shed their jackets, boots, mittens and snow pants and left them strewn on the floor in front of the door.

Grandma didn't care about the mess. She was relieved to see her kids and grandkids safe and sound.

The entire Jonsrud clan had gathered at Senior for the holidays. They swarmed the girls, getting them into warm clothes, feeding then a hot dinner and listening closely to their amazing story.

Abby brought out the mooring stone again and officially gave it to Grandma for Christmas. To help, Lexi stuck a candle in the opening on the stone, and Olivia lit the candle.

"Merry Christmas Grandma," Abby said. "I was going to wait until tomorrow to give it to you, but it seems like it's the right time to give to you now."

Grandma planted a kiss on Abby's head.

"Oh Abby, this is a wonderful gift," Grandma said.

Grandma gave hugs to Lexi and Olivia and then went around and gave hugs to each of her grandchildren and great-grandchildren.

"You know what," Grandma said. "This is a great Christmas. I know you feel badly about the sunken Viking ship, but that is nothing compared to being with family."

The girls felt better. They knew Grandmas was right.

But it was late. The family members split up to sleep at one of the three Jonsrud places on the lake.

It had been a very long Christmas Eve, with lots of highs and lows.

And, tomorrow was Christmas on Long Lake at Vergas!

Chapter 8: *Christmas bells and phones are ringing*

Abby awoke with the sun in her eyes. It was a bright day once again and the sunshine streamed in through the window above her bed.

"Meeerrrrry Christmas!" she yelled to anyone and everyone in Junior.

"Merry Christmas Abby!" her mom, dad and Olivia answered from below.

Abby sat up quickly and looked at Olivia's bed. It was empty! Olivia had gotten up before her! Wow, Abby thought—it must be Christmas or maybe even April Fool's Day!

The Jonsruds had a quick breakfast before heading to Senior to celebrate Christmas with everyone else.

On their way to Senior, Jon called Sheriff Carly and told her what had happened the day before. Sheriff Carly knew the girls from last summer when they had solved the mystery of the laughing loon.

Still, the sheriff said as Duncan had predicted—that in this case, "position was 9/10s of the law."

"I'm sorry Jon, but there is no proof that your girls were the ones who found the ship—if there is one," she said. "And if Duncan's buoy is directly over that ship, it is evidence that supports his story not their story. The girls need some other evidence to prove their story against his story."

"Well, thanks anyway Sheriff," Jon said and he and hung up the phone.

Shortly after, they arrived at Senior.

It was a beautiful, sunny Christmas day. Christmas lights twinkled across the deck and in the single blue spruce pine tree in the center of the sprawling lawn. Still no one was outside sledding, cross-country skiing or skating as they usually did on Christmas Day at the lake.

All of the Jonsruds were inside Senior, huddling next to the television set and watching the news.

The big story of course was about Duncan finding a sunken ship—perhaps a Viking ship--in Long Lake at Vergas.

They could see on the TV that a news reporter was interviewing Duncan right out on Long Lake.

Lexi ran to the window and saw in a distance that there were a number of people on the lake at the location where they had found the ship.

"Look! You can see them out there now," Lexi said.

"I don't care," Abby said. She was so mad that she was playing "Angry Fish" on her dad's cell phone.

"Yeah, I have studied Viking history for a long time, especially through books and the museums in Chicago, Detroit Lakes, Alexandria and Moorhead," Duncan continued in his interview.

"A few days ago, some girls told me about a stone they had discovered that indicated an ancient Viking ship may be around these parts."

Boy, Duncan was good at making up a story.

"I decided to begin exploring. And as luck would have it," I located the ship last night!"

The Jonsrud family booed Duncan's story. Abby was so mad she tossed her dad's phone and it landed in his full cup of coffee.

Splash!

"Oh Dad, I'm sorry," Abby said. "I didn't mean to wreck your phone."

She fished out the phone from the cup and handed the dripping phone to her dad.

"Well Abby, you know better than to throw a phone around, but in this case I understand your frustration," her dad answered.

Jon could see Abby was on the verge of tears.

"And Abby it is okay," he consoled his youngest daughter. "Your mom and I both bought waterproof phones, remember?"

"Yeah Abby—you know--they can take a dunkin' and keep on callin'," Terry said with a laugh.

Abby began to smile a bit and everyone laughed at Uncle Terry's joke.

Well, everyone laughed, except Olivia.

Olivia jumped up and ran to her dad.

"Dad, we have to call the sheriff back right now!" she hollered.

Although Jon didn't understand what Olivia was thinking, he could tell she was serious. He called the sheriff and handed the phone to Olivia.

"Sheriff Carly, can you meet me at the spot where Duncan says he found the ship?" Olivia asked. "And please drive your squad car on to the ice. We need your electronic equipment!"

She hung up her dad's phone and turned around to see the rest of the startled family staring at her.

"Come on everybody—there is no time to waste," Olivia ordered. "We are heading out on the lake to claim our discovery!"

Boots, mittens and snow pants flew through the air as the Jonsruds tossed belongings to each other and scrambled to get dressed to go outside.

Once outside, the 50 members walked, skied, and snow-mobiled across the lake to where the local crowd was gathered.

Sheriff Carly was pulling up in her squad car at the same time the Jonsruds arrived at the lake spot.

"Sheriff Carly, you said you agreed with Duncan when he said that position is nine tenths of the law, right?" Olivia asked.

Olivia then asked, "And Duncan you still believe that, right?"

"That's right, Olivia," the sheriff answered.

"Sure it is, kid," Duncan said.

Duncan was feeling large and in charge. And he thought it would look good for a museum director to be nice to children in front of the crowd.

"Okay then. Well, Sheriff, please turn on your GPS phone tracker," Olivia said with authority.

"I'm not following you Olivia," Sheriff Carly said. "Why do you need me to track a cell phone?"

"Sheriff if you turn on your GPS system, I believe that you will locate a beeper directly below us. And you will find that it's my mom's phone right next to the ship below us," Olivia said. "I dropped it last night when Duncan invaded our fish house after we discovered the sunken Viking ship!"

There were murmurs in the crowd in response to Olivia's assertion.

Abby started jumping around and pretended to make another nothing but net shot.

Lexi broke into a big smile and gave her cousin a big pat on the back.

Sheriff Carly leaned into her car and began to track Beth's phone number.

It took just a few minutes.

Sure enough. The "ping" that returned came from directly underneath their feet—90 feet below, next to the sunken ship!

"Well, I'll be," Sheriff Carly said. "Olivia, you are right. Your mom's phone is pinging right below us."

Led by the Jonsruds, the crowd began to clap and cheer. They were enjoying the sudden change of events.

In the midst of the noise, Sheriff Carly looked at Duncan.

He gulped and began to walk backward, but the crowd moved in around him. They wanted to be sure that Duncan didn't get away.

Seeing no way out, Duncan confessed.

"Alright, alright," he said. "These cousins are right—they were the ones that found the ship. I just kept following them because they were smart and I knew they were on to something."

"I guess they outsmarted me again," Duncan said and hung his head.

It was quite a turn of events.

The girls felt a little sorry for him.

"Well, okay then, Duncan I think I have to arrest you for filing false reports," Sheriff Carly said.

"You should be ashamed for trying to take credit for such an important discovery," she continued.

Duncan looked miserable and like he wanted to jump into the lake to get away from all the stares.

Lexi, Olivia and Abby looked at each other. They seemed to know what each other were thinking.

Lexi walked forward to Sheriff Carly.

"Sheriff," Lexi said.

"Yes, Lexi," the sheriff said.

"Well, it is Christmas," Lexi said. "Do you really have to arrest Duncan?"

"That's right Sheriff. Everyone deserves a gift at Christmas," Abby added.

The sheriff looked at the cousins, and then she looked at Duncan. She thought for a minute and then smiled. Just a little.

"You are right Lexi," Sheriff Carly said. "Everyone deserves a gift at Christmas.

The three cousins smiled at her.

Sheriff Carly began to unlock her handcuffs from Duncan's wrists.

"But, Duncan I don't want to have any more trouble from you. Keep your nose clean," ordered Sheriff Carly.

"Oh yeah, and Merry Christmas," she added with a smile and a handshake.

Duncan was stunned.

Then he slowly began to realize for the first time that the lakes area was pretty special with pretty special people.

"Ahh jeesh Sheriff, Merry Christmas," he said with a smile.

"And Merry Christmas to you Jonsrud cousins," Duncan said as he turned to the three girls and the entire family.

"This is a bigger gift for me than you may realize. Thank you," he said.

Lexi, Olivia, and Abby smiled back at Duncan.

They noticed that he didn't look the same; they saw a friendly twinkle in his eyes that had been missing before.

Before leaving the crime scene that had just turned into a friendly, Christmas scene, Sheriff Carly turned to the three cousins.

"Once again, you girls have done a great job of solving a mystery at Long Lake," the sheriff said. "And this time, by golly, that mystery may be 1000 years old."

"Merry Christmas to you and the whole family!" she said.

The crowd—including Duncan—clapped for Lexi, Olivia and Abby.

"A dream is a dream until it becomes reality." –Robert Asp, dreamer and builder of the Hjemkomst Viking Ship in 1973-1981.

Chapter 8: *Holidays end, legends continue*

The Jonsruds returned to Senior to celebrate Christmas, as wells as the discovery of the ship. The Herbsons, and even Duncan and Otto, joined them for a little Julebukking and snow shoeing through the woods.

Soon, it was time for the Jonsruds' tradition to gather around the Christmas tree in Senior's living room to sing Christmas songs before opening gifts.

The uniform singing turned into a noisy, exciting gift opening, filled with "wows" and "thank yous" across the room.

Could it get much better?

You bet it could.

After all, it was Christmas at Long Lake.

Once all the gifts were open, the kids were about to run into the basement to play with their new toys and games.

"Hey, hang on a second," Beth yelled through the noisy crowd.

"Yeah, hold on. There's one more gift to open," Jon said.

He tossed a bright red, shiny package across the room to Olivia and Abby. Although Olivia was about to catch it, at the last moment Abby jumped in front of her and nabbed the gift. Abby started her victory end-zone dance.

Everybody laughed as they watched Abby—even Olivia.

But after a few moments, in the middle of Abby's dance, Olivia hip-checked her sister and then grabbed the gift when Abby fell laughing on to the couch.

The girls giggled, but they were surprised that they had another gift.

And then it hit them.

They began to tear off the paper.

You guessed it.

They had finally received their very own cell phone!

"Wow—this is grrrrreat!" Abby squealed and jumped up and down.

Olivia started to jump up and down too, but then she slumped back to her knees on the floor.

"Now, what's wrong Olivia," her mom asked.

"Oh Mom, I'm grateful for the phone—thank you," Olivia said. "Only now I'm just thinking about Gretchen. Now she's the ONLY kid on our bus without a phone."

"Ohhh duuude, that's right," Abby said. "We have to help her. We better send a message to Santa and quick. I wonder if he texts?"

And Abby began to search online for his number while the whole family laughed at her plan of action.

It was a wonderful Christmas Day.

Over the Christmas break, the three cousins watched as local divers--including Monty, Brianne and Tricia—used special winter scuba gear to keep them warm and allow them to explore the ship.

Using underwater video cameras and lights, they were able to clearly identify that the cousins had discovered a real sunken ship.

With the help of Otto, Duncan, and experts from the US and Norway, the Jonsruds learned that the ship had indeed been petrified over time and that it was patterned after ancient Viking ships.

However, since the ship had been petrified and embedded in the rocks and sediments deep in the lake, it was impossible to dislodge the ship from the bottom of the lake and bring it to the surface.

Because of that, experts were unable to determine if the ship was 1,000 years old or only 100 to 200 years old.

In addition, it would probably take many years and experts to figure out if the writing on the slab was authentic and from 1,000 years ago.

Perhaps the full mystery would never be solved.

And maybe that was okay.

To help the community share the mystery and Viking legend, the cousins and Grandma donated Abby's mooring stone candle holder to the Detroit lakes Museum. Likewise, the Herbsons donated their slab with the writing on it.

Even though the community could not prove that the sunken ship was a from a Viking exploration crew from 1,000 years ago, the ship, mooring stone and slab brought international awareness again to the possibility of Vikings discovering North America before Christopher Columbus.

It was quite a Christmas for the cousins at Long Lake.

As the holiday came to a close, Lexi, Olivia, and Abby spent the last day at Senior helping Grandma take down decorations and the Christmas tree.

"Well, this has been one great Christmas, starting with Abby finding a mooring stone," Lexi said.

"Ahhh. Hey. You mean a candle holder," Abby interjected with a laugh.

"Yes, Abby. We all agree it is a mooring stone and a candle holder," Olivia said. "And Grandpa would be proud of you,"

Olivia hip-checked her sister.

"Oh you can be sure girls that Grandpa is very proud of all of you. And so am I," said Grandma.

It was kind of a tender moment for Grandma, but like all grandkids, Olivia couldn't stay in that moment too long.

"Well now, I wonder how we can top this mystery," Olivia said as she pulled the star from the top of the tree.

The three cousins and their Grandma laughed at Olivia's pondering.

Little did they know that in a few short months they would be up against another tricky, mystery—the mystery of the flying ghost in the Great Planes Museum.

###

Want to draw more pictures about the story you just read? Go ahead!

You can draw! Draw the cousins sitting by the Christmas tree as Grandma tells them about the history of Minnesota.

You can draw! Draw Lexi, her dad and Grandma in the snowy yard of Junior.

You can draw! Draw a mooring stone.

You can draw! Draw a Viking ship.

You can draw! Draw a snowmobile.

You can draw! Draw someone skating on a frozen lake.

You can draw! Draw a cell phone.

You can draw: What is your picture about?

You can draw! What is your a picture about?

You can draw! What is your a picture about?

You can draw! What is your a picture about?

You can draw! What is your a picture about?